Looking at Fish

Written by Ratu Mataira

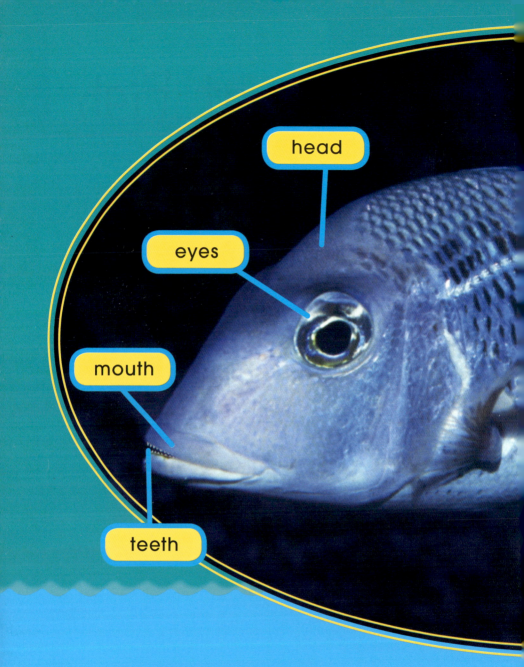

Look at the fish.

Look at this fish.
Look at the eye.

Look at the eye on this fish.
It has a big eye.

Look at this fish.
Look at the tail.

Look at the tail on this fish.
It has a long tail.

Look at this fish.
Look at the teeth.

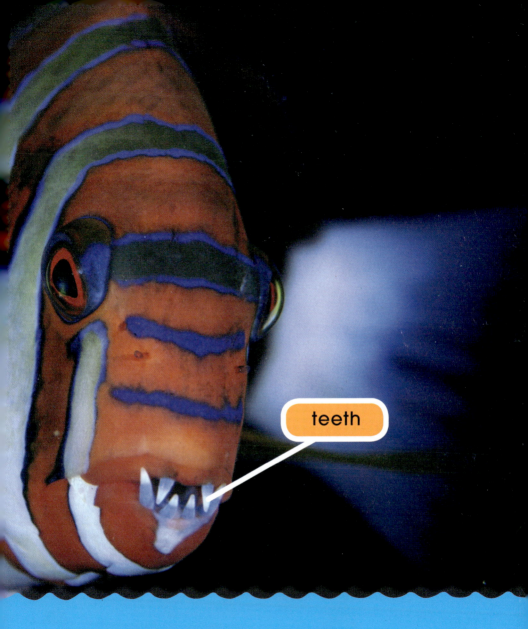

Look at the teeth on this fish. They are big.

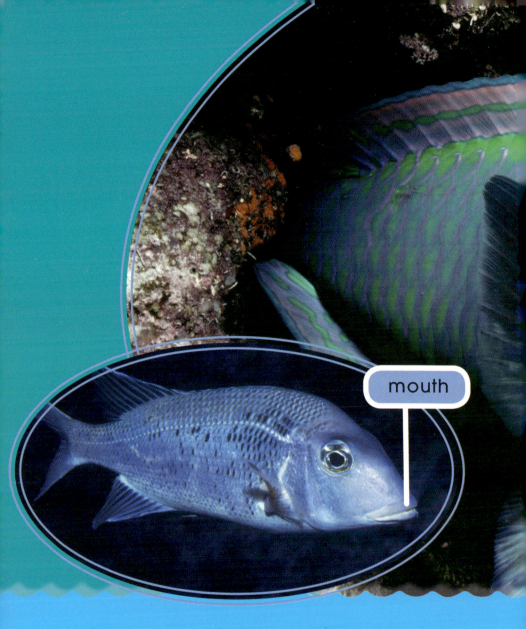

Look at this fish.
Look at the mouth.

Look at the mouth
on this fish.
The mouth is like a beak.

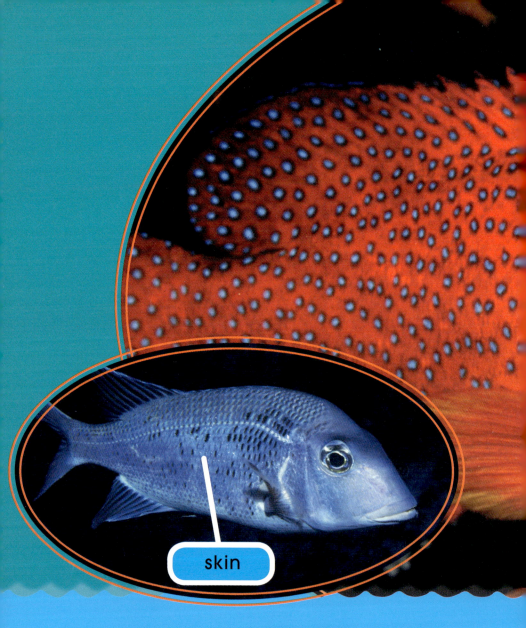

Look at this fish.
Look at the skin.

Look at the skin on this fish. The skin has spots.

Look at the fish.
Look at the skins.
They have spots.
They have stripes, too.

Index

fish
- eyes 4–5
- mouth . . 10–11
- skin 12–15
- tail 6–7
- teeth 8–9

stripes

Guide Notes

Title: Looking at Fish
Stage: Early (1) – Red

Genre: Nonfiction
Approach: Guided Reading
Processes: Thinking Critically, Exploring Language, Processing Information
Written and Visual Focus: Photographs (static images), Index, Labels

THINKING CRITICALLY
(sample questions)
- Look at the title and read it to the children.
- Tell the children this book is about some different fish.
- Ask them what they know about the ways fish can look.
- Focus the children's attention on the index. Ask: "What are you going to find out about in this book?"
- If you want to find out about teeth, which pages would you look on?
- If you want to find out about eyes, which pages would you look on?
- Why do you think a fish might have a mouth like a beak?

EXPLORING LANGUAGE

Terminology
Title, cover, photographs, author, photographers

Vocabulary
Interest words: tail, mouth, head, eyes, skin, teeth, spots, stripes
High-frequency words: it, have
Positional word: on

Print Conventions
Capital letter for sentence beginnings, periods, comma